DRAGON THIEF SERIES

<u>SEASON ONE</u>
Dragon Thief
The Chicago Job
The Poisons Book Job
The Vault Job
The Femme Fatale Job
The Scavenger Job

<u>SEASON TWO</u>
The Crown of Kingship Job
The Green Scroll Job
The Payback Job

The Poisons Book Job

A Dragon Thief Story

Dragon Thief

Book Three

Kat Simons

T&D PUBLISHING

THE POISONS BOOK JOB

For my boys.
Thanks for joining me on this life journey.

ONE

Myra slipped across the roofs of the Brownstones until coming to the roof she was aiming for. One that had a low wall and pressure sensors on the roof that were impossible to see if you didn't know they were there.

The Manhattan night kissed her cheeks with chilly air, the sounds of traffic over on Third a quiet hum. This neighborhood was exceptionally quiet at three in the morning, for Manhattan, but quiet in New York wasn't technically quiet. A couple of dogs barked a few streets over, which meant at least two people had to take their dogs out for walks at this time of night. She loved animals, but this is why, if she were to get a pet, it would be a cat. They could pee on their own while she was out working.

A cat burglar getting a cat might be clichéd, though.

The roof she needed to cross was wide and mostly empty, unlike the one she was standing in which was covered in raised stones boxes filled with plants and had a nice set of patio furniture and an outdoor grill. There were even trellises with ivy growing over them, though the ivy was mostly dead at the moment, given they were rolling into winter. The roof she stood on topped a Brownstone owned by a family that sent their two twin girls to private school and had parties up here that they claimed were for family but an awful lot of the mother's associates from the big accounting firm where she was a partner got invited.

Currently, the entire family was out of the country for a ski vacation, and the staff didn't spend the night. Which made this building a safe place to work from.

The roof Myra was aiming for was a wide-open square but for the small raised hut that led inside to the stairwell. The gray stone tiles on the roof looked ordinary and harmless. But her research confirmed they were sensitive enough to detect a pigeon landing on them. Which was probably annoying to the people who had to monitor the activity because there were a lot of pigeons in the city.

She pulled a hook and wire from a pocket of her jacket, and using a little spell to ensure the hook landed against the raised hut on the first throw, she swung and tossed the metal barbs, catching a sharp lip of the hut. She tied off the other end of the long wire to a metal loop fixed into the accountant's roof, a metal loop used to chain the grill down most of the time—for some reason, the residents hadn't bothered chaining the grill last time they'd used it. Maybe they'd assumed no one would try to steal it from off the roof?

There was an irony there since she was an actual thief but *wasn't* going to be stealing the grill. She had something a little different in mind.

She grabbed the wire, her gloved hands protecting her skin, and swung up so her legs hooked over, stretched out so she could use her feet to help her shimmy along the wire. Dangling over the motion sensor tiles, moving fast along the thin wire, she mentally asked all pigeons in the area to stay away for the next fifteen minutes.

The painting she was here for wasn't hanging on any of the walls inside the five story Brownstone. It wasn't kept inside a vault either, which was amusing to her. It was tilted against a wall in a closet on the third floor, one of many gently stacked into the closet, waiting for its rotation when it actually would get a position on a wall somewhere.

The Brownstone was owned, outwardly, by a small agency that claimed to represent artists in the city. Supposedly, all the art inside the mansion consisted of clients' work either given to the agency as a gift, or donated to the agency for resale. In point of fact, most of it was stolen from clients who were having trouble paying rent and buying groceries because their "agents" couldn't get them gallery showings or sell any of their work for more than a pittance.

Myra liked artists. It was a strange, but probably predictable thing, for a thief to have a soft spot for the people who created the things she stole. She never actually stole things from the artists, though. She stole things from the rich people who bought the artists' work.

Or in this case, stole the work first.

And this particular piece was worth a fortune according to an appraiser Myra sometimes worked with, but the agency had told the artist it was only worth a hundred dollars and they were being generous giving her that much. The artist was a single mother about to be evicted. Myra really didn't like that. So here she was, breaking and entering, not for her own amusement this time, but to help an artist out.

She might be a thief, but there were lines. And standards. And she had no compunctions about stealing from other thieves.

The hut was sturdy enough so that when she crawled on to it, it didn't even groan under her weight. Leaving the hook in place for her escape, she used the same lip that held the hook secure and folder herself over and down, hanging in front of the locked door without touching the tiles. Once she was certain her handhold wouldn't collapse, she released one hand and used a little spell to open the door. She could pick the lock in a pinch, but the spell finessed the lock in twenty seconds, saving her time.

Despite the pressure tiles all over the roof, the lock itself wasn't complicated. And the interior of the hut wasn't monitored or alarmed.

Sometimes thieves had blind spots. She liked to take advantage of those.

She slipped downstairs to the closet containing the piece she wanted, the house dark and quiet. No one actually lived here. This was a glorified warehouse and, when necessary, a fancy sort of office for the agency. The head of the agency, a man whose nasal voice irritated every last one of Myra's nerves, entertained wealthy clients here when he had something to sell, and intimidated eager artists here when he was trying to rope in a gullible aspirant.

When not in use, the place had a decent security system in place, but it was focused on entrance and exit points. Windows, doors, the roof. There was an elevator that was locked down when no one was using the house. And the first two floors had cameras in place that could be turned on remotely—and were during events so the agency's security team could monitor and spy on potential clients and customers.

But on the top three floors, the security was limited to doors and windows. A weird system, but it worked for her.

The lock on the storage closet was a cute little biosensor thing that didn't stand up to her spells and lock picks for more than thirty seconds. It tried, though. She was in and out of the closet in moments, waving her fingers over the locks to spell it sealed again.

Locked room mystery, she thought as she hurried back up to the roof.

The hardwood stairs didn't creak under her feet, but they might have if she hadn't had on her specialized shoes, a bit like ballet slippers that were almost like walking in socks, and had a little spell in the sole that helped dampen sound. She'd watched the building all day and knew it was empty, but better to be safe than sorry.

She tucked the painting into the small black nylon backpack she wore, which was just large enough to fit around the frameless one foot by one foot canvas, then opened the door onto the roof and reached up for the wire still taunt overhead.

She didn't scream when someone touched her gloved hand. But it was close. Years of training and practice keeping the surge of adrenaline spiked by irritated surprise from erupting out of her mouth. She looked up, prepared to run back into the house and escape through her alternate exit point.

Then cursed under her breath and shook her head, scowling up at the dragon shifter prince casually sitting on the hut above her.

Two

Christopher sat on the roof of the hut, his legs crossed, his huge wings tucked up against his back so that all Myra saw of them were the joints rising above his bent head. His blue eyes gleamed in the darkness, catching light from the surrounding buildings where a few windows were lit even this late at night. His dark hair ruffled in the cold breeze, calling attention to the fact that he was shirtless—what she was starting to think of as his flying uniform—the purple and yellow scales over his chest and the wings giving away his nature.

He was a huge man when standing, but like this, and from her current angle standing beneath him trying hard not to step out onto the motion sensor tiles lining the Brownstone's otherwise empty roof, it was hard to see. He needed a shave, she noticed, evening scruff darkening his jaw and almost, but not quite, obscuring the scar there. He had another scar on his forehead, neither of which she'd ever asked him about, though her curiosity was peaked.

He wasn't what most people might call handsome. Compelling was the word she used for him. Something about the arrangement of his features fit together to capture attention when all those individual elements should probably have looked awkward, maybe even ugly on a different man.

On this particular man, everything just worked.

She sighed. "What the hell are you doing here? I'm working."

"You've been avoiding me," he said, his voice quiet even though there was no one around.

"No, I haven't." Except she really had been.

"Why?"

"I'm working. Can we talk about this another time?"

"I'm here to help."

"Help?"

He nodded toward her back, where the canvas she'd just stolen was carefully concealed inside her black nylon backpack.

She narrowed her eyes up at him. "Is this because I'm helping a woman in trouble?"

He shrugged and glanced away but the darkening color along his cheekbones delighted her. He was ridiculously sweet about this kind of thing.

"Damsel in distress," she murmured.

He had a real soft spot for them. Got him into trouble all the time apparently. She thought it was adorable.

"Did you get the painting?" he asked.

She tucked her chin. "Did you really just insult me that way?"

"Sorry." He reached down for her hand.

She grabbed his thick forearm and let him lift her—with such ease it made her stomach flutter—up onto the top of the hut. She settled next to him, her legs dangling over the roof. "What was your plan?" she asked.

"To guard your back and then fly you off the roof to wherever you needed to go."

"Decent plan." And would save her time. "But you probably should have discussed this with me. Ahead of time."

"You've been avoiding me," he repeated.

"No. I haven't," she repeated, the lie slipping out on easily faked offense.

"What are you going to do with the painting?"

"Hand it off to my appraiser, who will sell it and then ensure the artist in question gets the full amount. Less a small fee for me and the appraiser, of course. But in this case, we're both only taking a nominal fee. The artist deserves a good payday after her agents stole so much from her."

"Does your appraiser have a buyer in mind?"

"Would you buy the painting if she didn't?"

He didn't answer but he did hold her gaze.

She grinned. "There is a buyer waiting. But it's sweet of you to offer."

"How much will the painting get?"

"Four million, give or take."

He nodded. "Good. Let me know if the buyer balks at that price."

"I will." She tilted her head and smiled softly at him. "You're entirely too sweet to be the dragon king's son."

He rolled his eyes, but that charming color darkened his pale cheeks again. "Can I see the painting?"

She shrugged and pulled her backpack around, unzipping it enough to show him the canvas.

The square, one foot by one foot, painting was a portrait of a child playing in a garden. The technique was exquisite, photo realistic but with an odd color palette that gave it an almost fairy-like quality. And it was that ethereal element, combined with the photorealism, that had made the work so valuable to collectors. Which the artist didn't realize. Because her agents were crooks.

"Beautiful," Christopher murmured.

"Definitely. And the buyer will treat it, and the artist, with the respect this piece deserves."

"I didn't know you had a soft spot for damsels in distress, too."

She snorted. "Nothing like yours."

She replaced the painting into her backpack and slipped the pack over her shoulders. Then she unlatched her hook and murmured a little spell that released the tied end of the wire from the neighboring roof. The wire snapped back fast, but not quite fast enough to avoid the pressure plates. The first few tips of the wire against the stone didn't produce any reaction. But at the last minute, the wire smacked against a stone, just before retracting fully.

"Oops," she said as she heard the alarm inside the house going off. A similar alarm would be going off at the agency's security office, where a sleepy but diligent guard would be turning on cameras to see if a pigeon was having a party on the roof.

At least, she hoped the guard thought this was a pigeon-related alarm. She folded and tucked the hook into one of her many vest pockets and stood, balancing on the small metal roof. "Time to go," she said.

Christopher rose to his full height which was very impressive and always made her tingly. She had a real soft spot for tall men. He snapped out his wings and she jumped up into his arms. He caught her easily and without comment. When she had her arms around his neck, he crouched low and then launched himself upward, leaping high above the Brownstones. He brought his wings down hard in two strong beats, catching the air currents, circling them up higher and higher until the island receding below, looking more like an elaborate model of a city than a real city beneath them.

He took them so high, the air was cold and thin, but his body heat kept her warm. When he'd flown a few miles from Murray Hill, and the site of her theft, he dropped back closer to the rippling skyline of high rises, moving them smoothly through the canyons created by buildings as he headed toward Central Park.

"Did you really come tonight just to help me steal a painting?" she asked, studying the side of his face as he stared out over the city lights.

"Not just. But I did want to help with this."

"Don't tell me, your father has another job for me?"

His gaze flicked to her, then out over the city again. "My father has another job for you. If you want it."

Did she? The dragon king paid very well. But the last job she'd done for him had been…irritating. Did she want to risk that sort of irritation again?

"Is it a real job this time? I'm actually going to be stealing something and not…whatever that last job was supposed to be?"

"That's what he says," Christopher hedged, not meeting her gaze.

She pursed her lips and considered her options. Saying no to the dragon king was probably a bad idea. But she no longer owed him anything, so she'd only be doing this because she wanted to. The pay would be good. And it was entirely possible the job would be fun.

The fun part was the real trick for her these days.

She gave a brief nod. "I'll hear him out, then. Not saying I'll take the job. But I'll listen." She gave a little wave. "Have to take care of tonight's acquisition first, though."

"I can take you to him tomorrow night. Will that give you enough time?"

"Tomorrow night will do."

"And maybe then you'll explain why you've been avoiding me."

She pressed her lips together so she wouldn't point out again that she hadn't been avoiding him. Because she had.

And it was because of his father.

THREE

She met Christopher in the open courtyard at the center of Columbia University. It was as good a place as any, because she was still hesitant to let him know exactly where she lived. Not really for his sake. But because she didn't want his father to know.

The dragons had been attempting to track her, but she was used to going unnoticed and slipping away from people. That was part of her job. Her thief magic helped as well because she could hide her scent. This came in handy whenever there were shifters of any kind around.

Dragon shifters had very keen eyesight, though. The kind of eyesight that could pick a human out of a crowd on a sidewalk while they were soaring high above the skyscrapers. That was something she had a harder time hiding from. But if they were in that crowd with her, they couldn't pick out her scent from the other humans surrounding them. And since the dragon king was trying to do this in a low-profile way, he kept sending his dragons in human form to follow her.

She was delighted by the fact that they kept losing track of her. Less excited by the fact that Christopher *could* track her. That he'd found her last night, even though she'd been working. She had no idea how he'd managed it, and that was the worrying part. Also the reason she picked Columbia as their meetup point. She had a feeling he might already know where she lived, but she wanted to keep the illusion going that she still had some secrets from him.

The night was cool but not too cold. That sort of mild, late autumn temperature that made for nice night walks, the soft glow of the city not far away. The courtyard in front of the Low Library was quiet at this time of night when college was out of session for some sort of break. The courtyard itself was lit by very dim streetlamps, softer and pinker than the orange lights on the sidewalks, giving the white stone columns and steps up into the library a glow.

Christopher was waiting for her, sitting on the marble steps, his blue eyes gleaming with a faint purple as she approached. He didn't stand, but waited for her to sit on the step beside him. He was such a tall man, she got the impression he often made himself seem smaller to keep from intimidating the people around him. Unless he wanted to intimidate those people, of course.

Myra didn't mind his height. In fact, she quite liked it. Which definitely complicated things. And made a lot of fluttering and tingling happen whenever he hovered over her.

He was wearing his "flight" suit, which tonight meant he had on dark cargo pants with side pockets that looked empty—what a waste of pockets—but no shirt and no shoes. He really didn't seem to like shoes very much. And the shirtless thing meant he intended to do the partial shift to give himself wings without changing any other part of his body.

One day, she hoped he'd show her his full dragon. She hadn't asked yet. Any more than she'd asked about his scars. And she wasn't going to ask tonight.

Instead, she went right to the point. "Your father waiting?"

"Impatiently. He didn't understand why this meeting couldn't take place last night."

"Because I'm not a dragon who comes at the king's call."

"I did point that out to him."

She grinned. "Figured you did. He hated that, didn't he?"

"To the depths of his soul."

"I'm not going on another wild goose chase," she repeated. "Not doing what we did last time. I hate being used. He crossed a line. I have one more line for him, and if he crosses that, I'm done doing anything for him."

"Fair enough." Christopher stood in a smooth, graceful flow of muscle and sinew that was just rudely sexy and stretched his hand out to her.

She took his hand and used his muscles to leverage herself up and directly into his arms. The fact that he didn't even blink at her suddenly jumping up onto him, that he just caught her automatically, did funny things to her. Made her soft and happy and fluttery in ways that were so so dangerous.

He held her gaze for a long moment as he cradled her close to his chest, and she didn't flinch away from that look. But the longer he held her, the longer he studied her face, the harder her heart pounded. When his gaze dropped briefly to her mouth, it took willpower not to lick her lips. They'd kissed once. Well, technically twice that same night. And it had been a very very good kiss.

She wanted to revisit that kiss. She knew he did, too.

But…

It was that internal "but" that kept stopping her. Not because it existed, but because she wasn't entirely sure what it meant. "But" what? She didn't truly understand her own hesitance. She knew it had something to do with him being the dragon king's son. And the dragon king being an ass who seemed to think he could lay claim to her, command her the way he commanded his cohort. This summons was just another reminder that the king *wanted* to be able to claim her as part of his cohort even if she wasn't a dragon.

She didn't like that, didn't like the position it put her in. And kissing Christopher would complicate that situation. She knew instinctively it would.

Unfortunately, self-preservation instincts did not stop her from wanting to kiss him again.

He blinked suddenly, his gaze jumping away from her face. Then he crouched and launched up into the air. His wings snapped out suddenly, the shift so quick, the appearance of his wings so sudden, she gasped.

He spiraled up high over the buildings, leaving her dizzy, her stomach dancing. All of it thrilling, like riding a roller coaster. She could do this with him all the time.

That was another reason for the ill-defined yet definitely serious "but" in all this.

They banked over the northern edge of Central Park, before Christopher headed to the top of Manhattan, to the dragon king's hold.

The mansion was a large complex tucked into thickly wooded lands. The king had no immediate neighbors, though land in Manhattan—anywhere in Manhattan—was at a premium. The mansion itself was a vague cross between a castle with its turreted towers and low retaining walls along the roof, and modern, with its funky architectural arrangement of box buildings and open glass walkways leading between section of the mansion.

The roof of the main building was huge, and flat, with a large grassy area on one side for the youngling dragons to land, and a large stone area on the other side designed to allow fully shifted adult dragons to land, one at a time, with ease. One at a time for defensive purposes. Easily because this was the seat of the king's power, the place the cohort aggregated when they needed to.

The place had been designed to be dragon friendly in every way. Even the proportions of the interior of the mansion were designed with dragons in mind, with the ceilings being that bit taller and some of the corridors wide and high so one of the cohort could walk through in his dragon form, wings tucked against his sides.

Myra's eyes were watering a little as they landed on the roof. Christopher had flown here faster and higher than he usually moved with her, and the air at that altitude had been cold and sharp. She didn't mind. She wanted to get this meeting with the king over with.

"Any idea what he's going to ask me to do?" She brushed her tears away as Christopher set her on her feet on the stone roof. He folded his wings against his back, but didn't shift them away.

"He didn't see fit to explain the job to me. Just…asked me to check in with you about doing it."

"Asked?" She snorted.

Christopher led her past the open, exterior metal gate that would come down if the mansion needed to be sealed off for any reason, and through the elaborate double wooden doors beyond that opened into the mansion. They were huge, those doors, and decorated with carvings and symbols she wasn't familiar with, all inlaid with precious stones, all of which she was familiar with.

She wouldn't attempt to steal any of them, though. Even when she'd broken into the dragon king's hoard on a bet, she hadn't intended on stealing anything valuable. Just a small token to prove she'd done it and win her bet. And she'd intended on putting the token back. A thief only stole from the dragon king at her peril. Only her dumb luck that they caught her before she'd escaped. She had no intention of giving the king any more influence in her life by stealing something else from him. But she did admire all the lovely, winking stones imbedded in the dark wood as Christopher pushed opened the heavy doors with shocking ease and led her inside.

A large ramp led from the doors down to the top floor of the mansion. From there, Christopher walked her directly to the king's throne room. The corridor was lined with slick white marble threaded with gold that sparkled in the lights cast by overhead Venetian glass chandeliers. The audacity of having glass chandeliers in a corridor where a full-grown dragon might walk was, she had to admit, pretty impressive.

The whole mansion had a vague scent of dragon to it, a mix of reptile, faint sulfur, leather and musk. It was hard to describe. Her sense of smell wasn't great, nothing like a shifter's, so she only noticed the undertone of musk and dryness that she associated with reptiles because the scent was so pervasive here. It wasn't a bad smell, by any means, just a lot of it in one spot.

And it hit her lizard brain hard. That lizard brain recognized a predator's scent and kept telling her to run away and hide under a rock so the giant flying death machines didn't find her.

As they neared the entry into the king's throne room, Myra thought her lizard brain might just be on to something.

FOUR

The interior of the dragon king's throne room was pretty austere for a place presided over by a dragon who had a hoard of wealth underneath the mansion. His throne was elaborate enough, a seat made of bones and gold and winking stones. Three bones rose above his head in arches that reminded her a little of rib bones, and they too were decorated in leaf gold with rubies and diamonds imbedded in them.

The rest of the room, however, was just a large bare, marble-lined space. The marble here a darker red color with lines of obsidian. And instead of glass chandeliers, the room was lit by a series of sconces lining the walls. They were electric, but designed to look like flickering fire.

Here, the underlying reptilian scent receded under a stronger smell of cleaning wax and bleach.

The place hadn't smelled so much like cleaner the last time she'd been here. What had happened that the audience chamber needed a good scrub down with bleach?

Probably something it was better she didn't know about. For her own survival.

She and Christopher stood shoulder to shoulder, or well, because he was so tall it was more like shoulder to thick bicep, but it was the thought that counted. They faced his father who sprawled on his throne in a more indolent slouch than he'd used last time she'd been here. Changing things up. Probably to keep her guessing. The bastard.

They'd been standing in silence since she and Christopher walked into the room. No one had greeted anyone. No words at all had been spoken.

Though she was still woefully ignorant of a lot of things about dragon shifters, she had finally started to do some research, as it looked like avoiding them going forward might be difficult, if not impossible. And she'd confirmed in that research that dragon shifters, at least the more common males, didn't have telepathy. There were rumors that one or two of the female dragon shifters did, but most of what was written about female dragon shifters was conjecture and hypothesis. There were only about twelve of them in the world. They mostly stayed away from other dragons, including each other. And they were so deadly, no one, not even dragon kings, went out of their way to change their minds.

Outside of those twelve females, most dragon shifters were male. There wasn't anything in the online searches she'd done about third genders or nonbinary or transgendered dragons, so she wanted to ask Christopher about that. But in the meantime, she had a few more details about basic dragon shifter biology, more than she'd known when meeting Christopher. And that included the fact that no male dragon shifter communicated telepathically. Not even kings. So the silence wasn't a conversation she wasn't able to hear.

The king was just being an ass.

The first one of them to break the silence was going to wonder if they'd lost. The longer this went on, the more certain she was of that. That they'd ended up in some kind of game the king was playing. A game that triggered her competitive instincts. She had no intention of speaking first. Let the dragons battle it out. And lose.

She did smile, though, when the dragon king's gaze fell on her. The family resemblance to his son was more obvious when they were standing in the same room. But the king was more conventionally handsome. Black, short curly hair with threads of silver through it, eyes that changed from blue to green depending on the lighting, a strong face. Though where Christopher's was long and narrow, the king's jaw and brow were more prominent. Thinner lips. The nose was different, too, she realized. She'd had more time to study Christopher's face since the last time she'd seen the king, and yeah, the nose was definitely different.

The king wore a small version of his larger crown, just a basic bejeweled diadem, nothing fancy—she nearly snorted at her own sarcasm—and instead of wearing elaborate regalia, he wore a black suit, complete with jacket and embroidered vest. During her last appearance in front of him, he'd worn dark trousers and an orange sweater, a color went remarkably well with his pale skin.

The casual wear, with the bejeweled crown as he sat on a throne of bone and gold and jewels had felt like a deliberate choice to throw her off. The change to a dark business suit felt equally deliberate. Though exactly what he was going for this time, she couldn't be sure. Nothing was ever entirely certain with the king. But when a man could shift to a building-sized creature that breathed fire, he could do whatever the hell he wanted.

"Thank you for coming, Myra," the king said, his head tilted in a graciously condescending way.

She held her smile, and her tongue. But the thrill of triumph that she'd *won* whatever game they'd been playing with the silence was very satisfying.

"I have another job offer for you."

Using the word *offer* was a choice. But she let it go. She wasn't going to reject his *offer* before she'd heard it.

"Curious?" he asked, his brow raised.

She was actually—irritatingly—curious what he wanted her to do. "Enough to still be standing here. Not enough to take the job without knowing what it is."

"I like you, Myra," the king said.

"Glad to hear it, your majesty." After their initial introduction, she wasn't so sure his statement was true, but she assumed his liking her meant he wasn't going to try killing her and that was always good.

"A book disappeared from my father's hoard a century before I was born," the king started.

She still had no idea how old the king was, just assumed he was old because he'd been around for a long time—though she assumed the threads of silver in his dark hair were affectations. But the mention of his father having a valuable hoard a century before he was even born was a pretty good indication that the dragons lived a very long time. According to the research she'd finally started, the males could live several centuries if they weren't killed. The trick was the not-being-killed part. Apparently, living to old age for a male dragon shifter was a real accomplishment.

"This is a magic book," the king said.

"Of course."

"It's resurfaced."

"Don't tell me. A wizard has it." There'd been a lot of wizards going around lately. The last thing the king had sent her after was supposedly held by a wizard. And Christopher had been stolen by shifters working with a wizard. She wielded magic herself, but she preferred to avoid wizards. She had been unable to do that lately. She did not like that turn of events.

"Not a wizard this time, surprisingly," the king said, his thin-lipped mouth tipping up at one side. Not quite a smirk, but almost one. "This time, it's a human."

"A human? That sounds…"

"Impossible?"

"Improbable." An ordinary human breaking

into a dragon king's hoard, even a few centuries ago, and stealing something that the dragon king had never found? Though, obviously this wasn't the same human. That human would have been dead for centuries. But the original thief was unlikely to have been a shifter or a wizard if a human had possession of the book now.

Maybe. Or maybe she was making assumptions. Lot of time in multiple centuries for things to happen.

"How'd the book end up with a human?" she asked.

"Sold. Apparently. From the original owner. In a private, underground auction. Which I wasn't invited to." His expression didn't change a lot, but his eyes narrowed, his nostrils flared, and a ripple of movement, a tightening, went through his jaw.

"Or you would have bought the book?"

"I would have…retrieved the book. Yes. Given it is my father's property."

"What's inside this magic book? Love potions?"

"Could be. Depending on your definition of a love potion. According to my father, and the legends, the book is full of formulas for various poisons. Magical ones that can do astounding things."

"Astounding things, like, kill stuff?" That was

generally what she thought of when she thought of poisons.

"Kill, yes. But what's poisonous to one being can be curative to another. Especially when magic is involved."

"Curative?"

"A poison that cures illnesses, for example. Or seals up a wound. Or one that extends the life of a human indefinitely."

"You actually believe any of that?"

"I haven't noticed any long-lived humans outlasting their natural lifetimes or swaths of people being mysteriously and miraculously cured from an outbreak of deadly disease, so either the legends around the book's contents are false, the poisons are generally just deadly instead of helpful, or the persons in possession of the book all these years never risked trying one of the spells. Probably for the best if they weren't a wizard."

Yeah, spells of any kind could backfire if you didn't know what you were doing. Even her small thief's magic could do more damage than good if she hadn't learned how to use it properly.

"But the book itself is said to bring great wealth to its owner. That sort of thing is harder to…discern. There have been many fortunes won and lost over my lifetime. Whether those fortunes were due to a magical book or not…" He spread his hands. "Impossible to say."

"How's the book bring wealth if not via a spell?"

He shrugged. "I'm only telling you what I've been told. Obviously, I've never even seen the book."

"But you want it back."

"I want it back."

"Because it was your father's?"

"Because it rightfully belongs to my family, in my hoard, and a human having it in their possession is offensive to me."

The way the king said human was like someone talking about dog shit on their shoe. Nice to know where she, as a human, stood in his opinion. "How much did the book go for?" she asked out of curiosity.

"A hundred million."

She let out a soft whistle. "Someone thought it was worth that amount. Someone thought the legends held water."

"Or just wanted to possess something that no one else had. There are those kinds of collectors."

That was very true. Those were the collectors she stole from the most because it was fun taking a thing they only had because they deemed themselves worthy of possessing it.

And the king knew that a fun, challenging job, especially one that stuck it to a rich collector, would be just the sort of job that tempted her. It was annoying that he had her number that way.

"So is the book currently in someone's mansion tucked safely away in the family vault with grandma's jewels, or did this human get creative?"

"Creative. It's on display. Private museum, security of the highest caliber, invitation only viewing."

"Which you were also not invited to?"

"Actually, I have received an invitation to view the book. Whether the new owner realizes it's a relic from my father's hoard is anyone's guess. But unlike the auction, I was not left off of this VIP list."

Wow, he was really annoyed by being left off the underground auction invite list. "Where's this private museum?"

The king made a small hand gesture, and a man Myra hadn't seen until that very moment stepped out of the shadows in the corner of the room and handed her a manilla envelope.

Myra raised her brows at the man. He was six foot and dressed in a suit, like the king, but was careful about the way he glanced at Christopher, keeping his head tilted down, and kept his gaze averted from the king's all together. He had no such compunctions about staring at her, though, but his expression was unreadable. Professional and neutral. She couldn't immediately tell if the man was a dragon shifter or not, but she suspected he was. Maybe the king's assistant?

"Thanks," she said, raising the large envelope in a little salute.

The man nodded and returned to the corner of the room without once making a comment.

"Everything you need to know is inside that envelope. Including a copy of my invitation so you'll know what they look like. Just in case."

"You still have the original?" She glanced down at the envelope without opening it.

"I intend on attending the viewing, yes."

"Groovy. Alright. I'm going to look through all this and let you know if I'm in. No guarantees. If I get this book back for you, it'll cost you." She named her fee, which was substantial. The book had sold for one hundred million. Her fee was a fraction of that amount. But retrieving something that valuable came with higher risks. Higher risks costs more.

The king didn't blink at her fee. "Done. Paid ahead of time?"

"Not until I confirm I'm taking the job. Then I take the full payment upfront." She didn't trust the dragon king as far as she could throw him. He'd paid her for the last job, but she wasn't prepared to assume he'd pay her this time if something went wrong. Full payment. Upfront. *Then* she'd do the job.

"The exhibition and private viewing are soon. I'll need to know if you're going to do this for me by tomorrow at the latest."

"More than enough time."

"My son will be assisting you again."

Not a question. Not an order either, she realized. Just a statement of fact.

She glanced up at Christopher. He didn't look away from his father but he gave a small head nod, confirming he would be helping her if she took the job.

He hadn't said anything during the audience. Hadn't tried to interfere in any way. Had neither tried to talk her out of the job nor tried to talk his father out of giving her the job.

Either he wanted the book returned to his father, too. Or he was going to save his attempt to talk her out of taking the job for when they weren't in front of his father.

"Tomorrow morning, then." She gave the king a quick, sharp head nod, and turned to leave without waiting for him to give her permission. It was a risky move. Dragon kings were notoriously prickly about that sort of thing. But she needed to make clear, again, she wasn't one of his dragons to command. And she no longer owed him anything. Not even deference.

Christopher moved up behind her before she'd gone more than a few feet. She had no idea if he'd paid his father a curtesy goodbye without words or just followed her. Would have been interesting to see which and see the king's reaction to it all. But better not to look back. Not now.

Now, she had to get somewhere safe, go through the contents of the manilla envelope, and decide if this was a job she'd take.

She nearly laughed at that. Of course she was going to take the job.

She just wanted to make the dragon king sweat.

FIVE

Myra watched the video feed streaming through to her phone from the pin-sized camera on Christopher's lapel, studying the crowd of mostly humans as he walked through them. Everyone parted the way for him, which was fun to watch from this vantage. A few people even looked up at him, startled, and scrambled to move out of his path in a way that looked very undignified in their fancy clothes.

"Are you scaring people on purpose or just being yourself and that's how people react?" she asked into the earpiece that connected her and Christopher so they could talk during this operation. Thanks to her pointing out his father had a plus one on the invitation, Christopher was there as himself, with his father, all on the up-and-up. Which had made one aspect of this job easier.

"I'm not purposefully trying to intimidate anyone," Christopher said, sounding monumentally annoyed. "But I'm not hiding being unhappy."

"Then you are intimidating everyone on purpose. Shame on you," she said softly and with a laugh in her voice.

Actually, he was playing his part perfectly. Lots and lots of attention on the king of the dragons and one of his sons stalking through the interior of this gallery. Well, the king wasn't stalking around. When Christopher swung around to give her different view of the room, she spotted the king holding court at one side of the huge open space, a dozen humans gathered around him, hanging raptly on his every word.

The old goat had to be loving that.

The gallery itself with inside an old Catholic church, one of the beautifully made stone buildings with flying buttresses and elegant stained-glass windows. The church was designated a historical building and so was preserved almost exactly on the outside. The inside had undergone some renovation over the years. The pews, altar, and lectern had all been removed. The interior was now mostly a wide-open ground floor with inlaid tile floors and decorative stone pillars running the long narrow length of the main room, separating the outer aisles from the interior of the nave.

A narrow gallery circled the main floor from two stories up, a vantage that would give a beautiful view of the tiling on the ground floor and allowed access to the three large wood and metal chandeliers that ran the length of the nave. At one stage there'd been a giant pipe organ up in that gallery, but apparently, according to the information the dragon king's assistant had given her, the pipe organ was out being refurbished and rebuilt from a state of extreme decay.

The fact that the currently owners of the gallery intended on bringing the pipe organ back made her happy for reasons she hadn't tried to explain to Christopher when he'd asked. She just liked when old things were still valued and taken care of—or at least returned to their former glory and *then* taken care of.

The artwork for this particular show was scattered around the ground floor. Some huge paintings were hanging in the large bays that dotted the exterior wall, where there had once been statues of saints behind stands full of burning candles. No candles now. At least not the kind that required fire. Around the open main floor, there were also wooden stands with various objects de art under glass cases. Most of the art, including the pieces under glass, were relics from the seventeenth and eighteenth centuries, the age of Enlightenment. So not as many saints and martyrs and a lot of realism and what people might see as modern art. There were also relics that looked like they belonged in an alchemist's lab.

There were also books under glass throughout the room. Large tomes covered in leather. Some opened to reveal the yellowing pages within, the ink faded but legible—she'd made Christopher stop at a few of them so she could get a closer look—and some were closed, revealing only the well-tended leather and any decorative inlays.

And in the center of the room, a very large display pillar with an empty glass case on top. The future location of the dragon's king's father's stolen magic book.

Future because it was currently being guarded in the crypt by some very large, burly human and shifter guards. About twelve of them. The fact that all that security was dedicated to a book when there were some extremely valuable paintings on the wall of that former church and at least one of the relics in the glass-topped pillars was worth almost as much as the book, just amazed Myra.

Oh, there was other security around. Plenty of alarms on the art and a number of guards casually strolling through the party as if they were guests. Christopher kept drawing their attention. And one of them was in the crowd around the dragon king, laughing at something the king said last time Christopher had swung the camera in that direction.

But the bulk of the security focus was on the magic poisons book that had once belonged to the dragons.

She was pretty sure, although not entirely certain, that the former owner of the book, the auctioneer, and the current owner of the book, all knew that the dragon king's father was the original owner. That was the reason he *hadn't* been invited to the auction but *had* been invited to the viewing.

She'd researched the human who'd bought the book. You spend one hundred million dollars on an old book, you are either a big-time collector of magical relics, or you know exactly what you're buying, and you know it's gonna piss off the king of the dragons, and you're doing *that* on purpose. But she hadn't learned much about the new owner. No one, not even the king, much to his irritation, had been able to find the actual buyer. Not even a picture.

That mystery was as tantalizing as the heist itself.

She'd been trying to see the collector all night, but they hadn't made an appearance yet. "Walk past the empty case again," she said into Christopher's earpiece. "Any sign of the book's new owner?"

"No grand entrance," he murmured. "If they're here, they've come in quietly and not made themselves known."

"Possible." But she doubted it. Waiting to reveal the book. Waiting to make an entrance. All this spoke to the purchaser being the sort who liked to make a splash. Who was dramatic and liked attention. Maybe the wrong kind of attention in this case.

Christopher's camera panned past the dragon king again as he returned to the center of the nave where the awaiting glass case stood under a spotlight. The king was still holding court, so to speak, but his gaze swept Christopher and his mouth turned down in a slight frown, before he let his charming smile out for his audience again.

Myra shook her head. Speaking of someone who liked to put on a performance.

The glass case under the spotlight remained empty. The crowds around it milled as if trying not to look like they were hanging out in the general area of the glass case, but they were definitely remaining in that general area so they didn't lose their position close to the case for the big reveal.

One man actually scowled at Christopher when he approached, as if he'd refuse to move out of the way and whoever was daring to try and dislodge him from his position was just going to have to pick a different route. Myra saw the exact moment the man realized Christopher was nearly seven-foot tall and maybe attempting to hold his ground against a man that size was unwise, followed closely by the realization that the seven-foot-tall man was, in fact, the dragon king's son. The man scrambled away, bowing his head in deference. And Myra had to put a hand over her mouth to keep from laughing loud enough for someone to hear over Christopher's earpiece.

"I can still hear you snickering," Christopher whispered as he approached the empty case.

"Sorry. But people's reactions to you are funny."

"Tiresome."

"Oh, the poor bored prince."

His snort was half amused, half irritated. She grinned even as she studied the case.

The platform that would rise up with the book on it was still locked into position. They hadn't begun the whole dramatic process of lowering that small platform into the pillar, down into the crypt where the book would be placed by one of those dozen security guards onto the platform, before the whole thing rose once again through the base pillar and into the glass case.

The case itself was sealed to the pillar. No way to actually get in or out of it without literally breaking the glass or ripping it off the stand. Which would be pretty obvious. And, according to the security specs she'd hacked yesterday, the unit was strong enough to prevent even shifters from tearing it to pieces. The pillar was embedded in the floor, also impossible to just lift out and fly away with. The tube through which the platform dropped into the crypt was made of titanium all the way down, and that titanium tube was also bolted into the stone floor of the crypt.

There was a single access panel that opened by a security code onto the titanium tube so that the guard could place the book onto the platform. Meaning that trying to snatch the book while it was in transit back up to the case would be impossible.

The only time the book wouldn't be encased in that secured apparatus, it was under the watchful eye of the security team inside a lock box chained to one of the guard's wrists. At least three of the guards were shifters—two lion shifters and an eagle shifter, which was interesting in and of itself —and the guard with the box chained to his wrist was wearing both bullet-proof clothing and a bespelled necklace that protected him from magical attacks. She'd watched the team walk into the church earlier that evening, before the party started. They were not messing around. A team of serious and professional guards, from an agency known for its efficiency and effectiveness.

Myra had seen less security surrounding the crown jewels of monarchs and priceless portraits in hyper-secure museums. She'd seen less security put into place in government buildings and embassies. The book was probably worth more than the hundred million the buyer had paid for it, and a hundred million was a hell of an investment even if that was all the book was worth, but the extreme levels of security meant the buyer knew the real value of the book wasn't in the price.

The real value of the book was in its relationship to the dragon king.

The fact the book was guarded against shifter attack as well as magical attack and mundane, ordinary human thieves just reinforced that impression.

Myra glanced at her digital watch. The watch, like the rest of her clothing, was all black, with a display face of pale blue that didn't throw up too much light and was difficult to see even with her night adjusted vision. A shifter might catch the glow, but she also had a little spell on the watch to prevent that. Her plan required precise timing. And not just her own timing, which she could keep track of without a watch, but coordinating that timing with Christopher. That meant using an actual watch.

"Almost time," she told him.

His grunt was his only response.

"I'm heading in now. Do not pay attention to me."

Another grunt.

She chuckled, tucked her cellphone into her pants pocket, and put on the special glasses she had had made just for this type of job. They had thick black ear bands and thin black rims around medium thickness lenses. Tiny rhinestones decorated the ear bands, a dash of sparkle when hit just right by the light.

Once on, she pushed a point on the ear band, and a tiny view of Christopher's camera display appeared across the inner left glass. From the outside, no one could see that display. There was a special coating for that, but she'd saved herself the expense and just used a tiny illusions spell so the lenses would look like ordinary, clear glass to anyone not staring through them.

She kept the display on, monitoring Christopher's view of the guests, as she finally got out of the plain, gray van she'd parked a block away and headed toward the venue.

Time for the show.

Six

Myra worked her way to the back door of the converted church where the catering staff were just starting to bring in the hors d'oeuvres after already circulating with flutes of champaign and wine.

She adjusted the collar of her black button-up shirt, straightening the long sleeves over her watch, and dusted her black dress slacks. Though it was cold outside, she hadn't worn a coat, so she could appear as if she'd been part of the staff from the start.

The small room at the back of the church, behind where the altar had been—she forgot what the area was called—was set up with long folding tables topped with temporary food warmers filed with silver trays of various tiny foods. The smell hit her the minute she slipped inside and might have made her stomach growl if she hadn't eaten a big dinner in anticipation of a fun night's work. There were spices and fried dough involved, though, so she might sneak a bite of something when no one was looking.

A man in a black cook's jacket stood behind the tables, directing two people as they loaded up large silver trays and handed them to the line of servers. The servers then pushing through a door at the end of the tables. The minute that door swung open, the noise of too many people talking at once from inside the church washed loudly through the back room, only to be cut back to a din when the door swung shut. Behind the food tables, a standing rack hung with a blue curtain half hid a plain black door with a surprisingly complex-looking series of locks running above the otherwise ordinary round doorknob.

A man with an empty tray pushed into the back room just as another of the servers started to head out. The noise drew everyone's attention as the two servers angled past each other.

Myra took advantage of the noise and inattention to blend into the line of servers waiting on food trays to take inside, adjusting her collar again and trying to pretend she'd been there all along.

The woman in front of Myra, a small, curvy Asian woman with her black hair knotted up in a bun on top of her head, glanced back, gave Myra a knowing look, then leaned in and whispered, "I won't tell them you were late, but you have to cover for me later when I need a smoke."

"Deal," Myra whispered. "Thanks. I've got you. How is it in there?"

"Crowded. Lot of rich twats. Few grabby hands you'll have to watch out for."

"Of course." Myra rolled her eyes and pushed her glasses up her nose.

Christopher, who could overhear the conversation through Myra's earpiece, made a strange sort of hissing sound that was a tad worrying. But since she couldn't see anything that might have caused that reaction through his camera feed, she ignored him. Which she would have had to do anyway with all the other people around.

"Hey, have you heard there are dragons in there?" the woman whispered.

"No shit? No one told me there'd be dragons tonight. What are they like?"

"Wild. Tall. The *king* is in there. And one of his sons."

"Oh fuck." Myra pressed her lips together. "What happens if I spill a drink on one of them?"

"Count on losing this gig and all future ones."

"Shit. Okay." Myra made a show of attempting to pull herself together, straightening her shirt and swallowing hard. "First time I've been in the same room with any dragons."

Christopher snorted. She ignored him.

"I've done it before," the woman said. "They're okay. Just, you know, don't piss them off."

That was very good advice. Advice she wished she'd given herself when she'd made the mistake of taking a bet and breaking into the dragon king's hoard.

She was handed a tray of tiny bites of food—she was pretty sure they were miniature empanadas, but they were so small it was hard to tell. Could have also been miniature egg rolls. As she headed toward the door into the church proper, she glanced briefly at the locked door half-hidden behind the standing curtain.

Then she pushed through the doors and into the din.

Each server moved into the throng and spread out to ensure maximum coverage of guests. She went in the opposite direction from where she knew—even without hearing his voice—that the dragon king held court. She didn't approach Christopher either, letting another server—the woman who'd warned her about the dragons—take his section of the gathering. A section where, Myra was pretty certain, her new friend would be safe from any "grabby hands" guests because Christopher would snap the wrist off of anyone disrespecting the staff.

Myra liked that about him.

She wound through the crowds, studying the people she'd seen earlier through Christopher's video feed. The dual view of seeing the venue in person and through his feed inside her glasses' lens gave her a pretty thorough impression of the place. When not filtered through Christopher's earpiece and camera, the noise was louder, the dim lighting from the overhead chandeliers carried more ambiance, the scent of so many different perfumes and colognes strong even to her ordinary human sense of smell, and the spotlight on the still empty glass case where the book would be seemed even brighter. Very obvious that something important was going to be in that display case. Eventually.

She subtly glanced at her watch. They only had a few more minutes.

Myra made her way past the display case, giving it a glance, but pretending to pay more attention to the guests as they plucked the tiny bite-sized pieces of food off her tray using the toothpicks sticking out of the food, leaving behind the minuscule bits of lettuce on which the food sat.

One guest turned suddenly and grabbed three of the bites at once, making a yummy sound that surprised Myra. She backed up a step from the man's gleeful expression and bumped into the currently-empty display case, setting one hand against it to hold her balance as she attempted to keep the food tray from clattering to the ground.

The case was solid as stone and didn't even wobble when she hit it, but a few people nearby gasped, and a man Myra was sure was one of the circulating security people stomped up to her and pulled her away from the pillar.

"Watch it," he hissed under his breath. "There are alarms on all these cases. The owners will be ticked off if you set one off on accident and cut the party short."

Myra quickly adjusted her glasses and nodded frantically.

The guard gave her a brief nod, took one of the hors d'oeuvres off her tray, and released her arm, giving her a gentle pat. "Just be careful," he murmured before weaving back into the crowd.

Myra did the same, angling away from the empty display case and the bright white spotlight on it. "Ah. He seemed nice."

"Focus on your job," Christopher murmured.

She chuckled. "My part is handled. How are you doing?"

"Almost in place."

Through the feed on her glasses, Myra watched Christopher approaching his father's location at the rear of the church, not far from the door where the servers were still moving in and out in a steady flow of full and empty trays.

A little wave of hushing and quiet murmuring moved through the crowd. Myra positioned herself with her back to the wall so she could watch the dais where the altar had once stood at the head of the church.

Gasps erupted around her as all the lights but the spotlight on the empty case dropped suddenly.

And when they came on again, a woman and a man stood on the dais, smiling like triumphant warriors at the startled yelps followed by loud cheers and applause.

Myra shook her head, stopped just short of rolling her eyes. So dramatic.

SEVEN

The woman standing on the dais at the top of the church was a medium sized older white woman with bright silver hair done up in an elegant twist. Her jewelry sparkled and winked in the chandelier lights. Diamond earrings, an emerald and diamond necklace, and a series of diamonds woven into her hair. All of which made Myra's thieving heart yearn. Dressed in a long emerald silk gown, the woman wasn't slim but she wasn't heavy either. And her silver heels gave her both stature and excellent posture.

The man next to her was dressed more austerely in a black suit, white shirt, and silver tie, though every bit of clothing looked tailored to perfection on his rail thin body. He was also white, with an expensive artificial tan, his hair a dark brown that didn't look like its natural color, and his features were cut sharply in a long face. Very few lines showed around his eyes and none appeared on his forehead or around his mouth. He was, Myra supposed, technically handsome, though the kind of handsome that required some maintenance and work to keep it up. And looked too artificial to her to be really handsome.

Unlike his companion, he wore no jewelry except for a substantial gold and ruby ring on his right pinky. A ring that drew Myra's interest almost more than the woman's jewelry.

As the crowd continued to applaud the dramatic entrance, the woman waved an appreciative hand, then gestured for everyone to quiet. Though the church was quite large, when the woman spoke, her voice carried throughout the venue, and Myra realized she was mic'd up and there were speakers in the rafters. The speakers gave the illusion that the woman was talking right next to her. She didn't even have to raise her voice.

"Welcome, welcome. I'm delighted to see so many distinguished guests grace our small gallery."

"That's the gallery owner," Christopher said into Myra's earpiece. "The man is her husband.

They aren't the ones who purchased the book at auction."

"You're sure?"

"Sure."

Huh. She'd been certain they were the purchasers. Or at least one of them was. The one thing none of them had been able to ferret out was the identity of the person who'd spent one hundred million on the book. The underground auction took anonymity seriously. The records Myra had been able to hack, which were surface because her hacking skills only went so far—she should probably find someone better at that to help more often but she didn't like working with other people—revealed a shell corporation as the buyer. They all knew that wasn't the purchaser. Myra didn't know this gallery owner on sight either. She'd never robbed this place before, which was a bit strange in hindsight, and there weren't any pictures in the records.

She realized as she let the woman's droning welcome speech wash over her that there were no cameras inside the church either. No phones snapping pictures of the big reveal. No press documenting the event. That might have been a dictate from the dragon king. There were no pictures allowed of the royal family. But not even a small contingent of press to document the event and carefully *not* take pictures of the dragons…? Seemed odd now that she thought of it. Explained why there probably weren't any pictures of the owners, though.

But if there were no pictures, how did Christopher know them?

"Been to one of their showings before?" she asked.

"A few."

Well. He could have told her that ahead of time.

The droning speech ended with a dramatic flourish of popping lights around the dais and some smoke slowly creeping out across the tiled floor. That was fun.

"The dragon has come," the woman said, her tone low and ominous.

Myra did roll her eyes this time. She just couldn't help it. "Well, you did invite two of them," she murmured. Christopher snort-laughed in her ear.

She searched the room for the location of the other servers, trusting Christopher and the king to be in their places by now. Most of the servers had stopped and were standing as unobtrusively as possible against walls, or pillars, behind the crowds so they wouldn't obstruct anyone's view. Just as she was doing.

The faux smoke reached Myra and spread past her, cold against her lower body. Definitely not dragon's breath, she thought. That was supposed to be hot.

A lot of show and drama, but Myra didn't mind. She liked a little show and drama. Especially when it helped her plan.

The two gallery owners moved down through the crowd, the crowd parting for them as they made their way to the still empty case. Its spotlight looked even brighter now, with the smoke catching in the light beam. The whole thing made a sort of haze around the case that looked very mysterious.

Myra smiled as she saw the little panel inside the case slip to one side. Here comes the prize. She set her mostly empty tray behind a pillar, checked her watch in the darkened corner, and started making her way around the edge of the nave.

The book rose slowly into the case, first the top corner, then inch by inch the rest was revealed. There hadn't been any images of this online either. Not even from the original underground auction house. Just a line item on a list. So this was the first time she'd gotten to look at the magic poisons book that had once belonged to a dragon.

It didn't disappoint. The tome was huge, easily

a foot wide and two feet long. Covered in a shimmery black leather that was so smooth it could probably be a mirror. On the front, in gold leaf, a symbol of some kind, nothing she could see clearly from her position near the edge of the crowd, but it was circular and looked like it required a lot of that gold leaf. In the middle of the gold symbol, a bright red ruby winked at the crowd like a drop of blood had dripped onto the center of the cover. All of it shimmered and glowed and sparkled.

There were no other outer markings on the book that she could see at this distance. But the black metal lock on the side of it was interesting. And the page ends had been coated in a dark red color she assumed was supposed to look like blood, same as the ruby.

That looked so much like a magic book it was almost ridiculous. If she were going to make a magic book of poisons, she'd make it look ordinary, plain, something no one would guess was an actual magic book. That puppy screamed *I'm a valuable and dangerous book*!

Although, maybe that was the point? And to be fair, it had once been in a dragon hoard. It might not have found its way there if it had been too ordinary looking.

Still, just to be sure… "That it?" she asked Christopher.

She looked across the crowd at him. He was easy to spot at nearly seven feet tall, a head over most of the people here, and he had taken his position by a pillar close to the display case but not right next to it. He glanced at his father, who'd come to stand closer to the case, his full retinue of sycophants in tow.

The king gave a little nod, without even looking at his son. Christopher said into her earpiece, "That's it."

Excellent. "I'm setting the lures," she murmured, continuing to work her way around the edge of the church. No one glanced her way. No one paid any attention to anything but the raised display case and the mysterious, magical book.

The woman who was the gallery owner turned to the king, which drew everyone's attention to him. He was good at being the center of attention, Myra noticed. He preened and puffed himself up even more and, because he was tall, looked down his nose at everyone. She wasn't sure if that was an exaggerated show for the crowd and for the sake of their plan, or if that was really him—but she suspected it was a combination of both.

"Majesty," the woman said. "What do you think?"

"Stunning," he said, and his deep voice carried throughout the crowd easily. Without needing a mic like the woman.

The gallery owner smiled. "It truly is. Worth every cent it earned at auction."

"And more," the king confirmed. "But as it's stolen property, it must be returned to the original owner."

Myra smiled. *You tell her, majesty.* Myra slipped past a series of valuable paintings and pressed more of her little button sensors against the wall, ensuring they were stuck in place before moving to the next display.

If Christopher had done his part, the display cases around the room also had those little sensors stuck to them. She'd placed the one on the poisons book's display case personally.

She did actually sort of trusted Christopher. He could have done it. But he was too obvious in this crowd.

The "sort of *trusted*" Christopher part of that thought was going to give her some feelings later that night when she looked back on all this.

By the time she reached the far side of the nave and was near the servers entrance again, the debate over ownership between the king and the gallery owner had reached a substantial volume, and every eye in the place was on the debate. The fact that the gallery owner was still smiling, even if her smile was a bit brittle, and her husband still looked mildly bored, meant they'd been expecting, maybe even hoping for, this show. It just added to the event. Otherwise, they wouldn't have invited the king.

Smoke still covered the tiled floor and had filled in the entire nave now. An added bonus Myra hadn't counted on. She glanced at her watch.

"Ready?" she asked quietly.

"Ready," Christopher said. He moved to stand just behind his father's shoulder, a very prominent location where he couldn't be missed.

And *everyone* in the room, even the servers, were staring at the scene.

Myra loved a good scene.

She counted quietly to ten. Then pressed a button on her watch.

And every piece of art in the gallery flickered and disappeared.

Eight

The gasps started near the king and Christopher. The first shout indicating something was wrong came from someone in the king's collection of sycophants at his back. "The book! It's gone!"

More gasps throughout the church. Then the yelling and shouting really got started.

"It's gone, too!"

"Where's the art?"

"What's happened?"

"Is it magic?"

"It's the smoke! They've rigged the smoke."

That last one was one Myra hadn't had on her bingo card.

The chaos and smoke and dim lights made it all so much better. People moving and shuffling around. The security guards in the room shouting for everyone to stay where they were. "*No one move!*" Except everyone was moving. Everyone but Christopher and the king, who stayed perfectly still, glaring at the crowds, demanding explanations even as the security guards swarmed around them.

The door back to the caterer's station swung open. Another stream of guards came bursting into the room. The dozen from the crypt. Myra smiled. The shifters flew past her, going right to the king and Christopher.

And Myra slipped through the door and back into the caterer's area. The cook and any staff who'd been back here had already hurried into the main part of the church when all the noise erupted. No one even back here having a smoke.

She slipped through the multi-locked door that had been left open when all the guards came charging upstairs. And why would they bother to lock it? There was nothing down there anymore. All the art had been upstairs, including the book. Which was now vanished.

She circled the stone stairs that led into the crypt, running her now gloved fingers lightly over the stone wall. It was even colder down here than it was outside, which was nice after the heat in the gallery. The air was a bit stale and musty, but not as moldy as she'd have thought for someplace called a crypt. And it was well lit and bright, the white stones reflecting the overhead fluorescents so the place felt a bit like an office building.

She shuddered at that.

The crypt itself was relatively small. A low-ceilinged room with stone floors and walls. Where once there'd been plaques for the dead buried there, the walls were now blocked by stacks of wooden crates and painting boxes. The specially designed, high tech titanium tube which protected the book as it rose up into its display case, the protective barrier that was supposed to prevent theft, was bolted into the stone floor at the very center of the room.

There was a lock on the hatch that allowed access to the interior of the tube, a simple number coded panel with raised push keys, metal and without any biosensors. And there was a small up and down button beside that.

Myra pressed the down button, rocking on her heels as she let her gaze travel over the small room. Christopher would bash his head on this ceiling.

She heard a little chu-chink sound from inside the tube. Then she hit a button on her glasses and the view of the chaos upstairs through

Christopher's video feed switched to a blue display that analyzed the lock panel.

Residual heat from the guard who'd entered the code to open the panel rose, allowing her to see four numbers had clearly been pressed. The code required five numbers so one of those four was a repeat. If she entered the code wrong once, she'd have twenty seconds to enter it right or an alarm would go off. Given the noise from upstairs, filtering all the way down here, she wasn't sure if anyone would even hear the alarm, but it would give away the game if they did.

She studied the heat signatures, the numbers pressed. And made a guess based on one number having a slightly higher signature.

A grating beeping sound when she got it wrong.

Damn. Okay. One more try.

She held her fingers over the lock pad and whispered a spell. The spell couldn't open the pad, but it could move her fingers true. It wasn't always as reliable as just figuring the code out herself, but she didn't have time to try and fail again.

Her fingers danced over the pad, pressing buttons. She smiled when she heard the lock give.

The panel clicked and lifted out of alignment with the tube, then with a quiet buzz moved to one side. Inside the tube, the platform from the case upstairs. With the magic poisons book sitting on it, the shiny black leather binding winking at her. The gold leaf and ruby in the center of the book's cover glittered in the bright crypt light.

She took off her cloth belt, gave it a shake. It opened into a sturdy, black cotton backpack. Only just barely big enough to hold the book, but it would do.

Clicking her glasses back to the view above, she confirmed things were still chaos and noise up there. Christopher stood just behind his father's shoulder, facing a guard Myra hadn't seen earlier —one from the crypt she was sure—and behind the guard, the gallery owner and her husband. Everyone but Christopher was pointing and talking in harsh, demanding tones. The guard had to hold his arms out to keep the woman from stepping too close to the king. And since he was her guard and not the king's, that was a telling gesture.

Myra grinned as she slipped the book from the tube and eased it into her backpack, then slipped the narrow straps over her shoulders. Heavy. But not as heavy as all that black leather and the winking ruby made it seem like it might be.

She closed the panel and sent the platform back up into the display case above. Then hurried up the crypt steps, listening intently, prepared to run all the way back down if she heard noise from the door. But all the noise and all the attention was still focused on all the missing art in the gallery.

The caterer's area was still empty when she slipped back out of the half open door. The servers and cook must be having a great time watching all that mayhem. She couldn't see any of them through Christopher's feed, but if she were an actual server, she'd have been in the middle of that room watching the drama.

Slipping out the same door she'd slipped through earlier to join the catering crew, she started to tell Christopher she was out when a puff a smoke to her right and the distinct scent of tobacco stopped her with her mouth half-open. Her server friend stood against the stone wall of the church, in the dark beyond the circle of light from the security lamp above the door, puffing away.

She motioned Myra over. "How's it going in there? Anyone kill anyone yet?"

In her camera feed, Myra could see some of the guards heading back in the direction of the catering area behind the altar, back toward the door leading into the crypt. Christopher turned slightly, keeping them in view long enough for her to confirm their direction.

"Everyone was still screaming when I slipped out," she said to her smoking friend as she leaned against the wall beside her, her backpack pressed into the stones.

The woman offered Myra a cigarette from a pack she had tucked into her jacket pocket. Unlike Myra, the woman was wearing a coat, an oversized black wool coat that looked a couple of sizes too big for her. Myra took the proffered cigarette and let her friend light it while keeping half her attention on Christopher's feed and some of her attention on the door to her left.

"Figured I could slip out for a smoke and no one would notice," the woman said. "Who d'you think figured out a way to steal all that art? That had to be magic, right? The way everything vanished?"

Myra shrugged. "Don't really know. Wizards, maybe? If it was magic, though, that was a big security hole, right? I mean, wasn't that book supposed to be magic or something?"

The woman shrugged and took a deep drag. "All I know is I still better get paid. My feet are killing me."

"Same." Myra took one long drag at her cigarette and let the smoke out slowly in a long stream as the back door swung open and slammed against the stone wall.

Both she and her new friend looked at the three men pushing out of the door, one of whom, Myra confirmed, was one of the lion shifters. They searched frantically around the narrow courtyard behind the church, then looked toward Myra and her friend.

"You ladies seen anyone come out this way?" the lion shifter asked.

He was a little shorter than the other two guards, broad and dressed in a black suit, black shirt and even a black tie. His sandy hair was cut short and his beard trimmed neatly. Not much about him screamed shifter until he sniffed the air, his head turning in a very not-human way as he scanned the area with his nose. That and the long narrow slit of his pupils inside golden eyes. His pupils whirled open as she watched him come farther out into the darkness behind the church.

Myra took another puff off the cigarette and blew the smoke into the air, leaning more heavily against the stones at her back. "No one but us," she said.

"Bad habit," the woman said, lifting her own cigarette. "Any idea what happened in there?"

"It's being handled." The shifter stayed a few feet away, his nose twitching, his nostrils compressing. "You don't need to worry, though. There's no danger."

"Thanks for that," Myra said. "Seems pretty crazy."

"Garet," one of the other men said, drawing the lion shifter's attention.

"Thanks for your help, ladies," the shifter, Garet, said, looking back at his companion. "I would recommend remaining out here or in the catering area until everything is settled." He faced them briefly. "You should have worn your coat." He nodded at Myra.

"It was so hot in there," she said, "feels good out here without it. But I'll be fine, sir. Thanks." Myra flashed her most innocent smile and let the smoke from her cigarette fill the space between her and the shifter, keeping her back firmly to the wall so her backpack wasn't immediately visible, its black straps blending into her black shirt in the darkness.

Garet nodded, his companion called him again, and he turned away, rushing around the church to the front of the building.

"What a mess," her new friend said. "Someone's gonna get fired."

"So long as it's not us," Myra said. She snubbed out the remaining half of the cigarette against the stones behind her. "I'm gonna take off. They're not gonna start serving again, and I don't want to waste a night getting questioned by those guards over and over again."

"You sure? They might get suspicious if you disappear before someone asks you what you were doing when it happened." She lowered her voice and said the last in a gruff, exaggerated tone that Myra took to be a joke.

She grinned. "I was questioned already, though, right? We both were by that guard."

The woman nodded. "True enough. Might take off in a minute myself."

"Good luck. Thanks for earlier, covering for me. And for the cigarette." She waved over her shoulder as she headed around the church, same direction the guards had gone.

"Hey," the woman called, "you forgot your coat."

Myra turned, though she kept walking backward. "Forgot it at home. Never had one." She waved. "Have a good night." And slipped around the church.

The front of the gallery was crowded with people in fancy clothes all talking over the top of each other while some of the security team tried to keep them from leaving. There was a lot of shouting and pointing and demanding and raised hands trying to hold back the tide. The guards who'd pounded out the back door, including Garet the lion shifter, were among the people trying to keep the guests from leaving. None of them looked her way.

She slipped down the road to the closest side street, then turned a corner. Once she was out of view, she took off at a jog that brought her several blocks to the south. She didn't bother returning to the van she'd left parked two blocks from the building. She could get that tomorrow. She hadn't left anything behind to point to her even if someone decided it was suspicious and searched it.

Instead, she headed to the bright green and white globe of light over the nearest open subway station. "Heading underground," she said to Christopher, glancing at her watch. "Illusions will cut out in twenty-six more seconds."

"I'm ready," Christopher murmured.

From his feed, she could see he and the king were still facing off with the gallery owners. She wanted to hang out long enough to watch their faces when the illusions broke. The buttons she and Christopher had pressed against the walls around the gallery, into the bases of the various display cases, all those temporary spells flickering out and all the "missing" art reappearing. She wondered exactly how long it would take everyone to notice the one and only thing *really* missing was the book. That everything else had just been covered by an illusion that made it seem like they were missing.

But she couldn't hang around and watch the show. She did get one last view from Christopher's feed as the various spells started to flicker out around the nave and the gallery owners standing in front of Christopher and the king turned in a circle, looking at the returning art, their mouths hanging open.

She chuckled as she slipped underground and hurried through the turnstile to make her train.

NINE

Myra met Christopher on a rooftop in Midtown, the same rooftop they'd landed on after she'd rescued him from his kidnappers those many weeks ago. And he'd rescued her from tumbling to her death. Though she didn't remember that part because she'd been hit by a wizard bolt and was unconscious for most of her fall.

She was looking out over the tightly packed skyscrapers, the lights inside windows bejeweling the skyline, noise from traffic below distant but distinct. Up here, the air was fresher, and colder as the wind cut through the canyons created by the buildings. The night had grown overcast, turning the sky a funny orange color as the clouds reflected the city's night light back down to it.

She heard the sound of his wings, felt the brush of air at her back from his landing. She didn't immediately turn to face him, instead leaning against the waist-high brick retaining wall circling the flat roof.

"Is the book safe?" Christopher asked, his voice quiet to match the late night.

"Got it stored. We can bring it to your father in a couple of days, after the chaos dies down."

"He'll want it tomorrow."

"He'll have to wait. He might be the dragon king, but that won't keep people from investigating. Especially when the stolen artifact just sold for a hundred million at auction. Better for him to have no idea where the book is, and even be mad about that, when the police do show up to question him. They'll buy his outrage better that way."

"Good plan. He'll hate it."

She grinned. "What happened once the art reappeared?" she asked, her attention still on the lights in the building across the street. She felt him come up beside her, saw him lean against the retaining wall next to her from the corner of her eye. He had to lean down a lot farther to reach it.

"Confusion and chaos. Exactly what you wanted."

"How long before they realized the one thing really missing was the book?"

"About ten minutes. My father got impatient and pointed it out."

She raised her brows. "Huh. That probably worked in your favor."

"It did. He roared about it missing and started shouting at the owners about their shoddy security. Made a huge scene, even bigger than the one he'd already caused."

"Perfect. He carries that energy into a meeting with the police, and we'll get away with this without a hitch." She tilted her head into a gust of cold wind blowing across her face. "The king was really good at his role in all this."

"I think he enjoyed it a little too much."

She chuckled. Finally turned to look at him. He was also staring out over the city. The wind blew through his messy dark hair. In profile, his angular face took on a sort of nobility, the kind of thing she'd seen in marble statues in the Met. He was still wearing the dark dress slacks he'd worn to the event, but he'd stripped off his shirt and he had taken off the loafers he'd worn earlier in deference to humans' preferring for footwear at fancy parties.

His wings weren't out, though. He's done the partial shift and looked fully human now. Even the purple and yellow scales that covered his chest and shoulders when he shifted to just having wings were gone. He looked like an ordinary, handsome, very tall man. Who should probably be cold standing around with so few bits of clothing on.

She didn't bother asking him if he was cold. His dragon metabolism kept his body temperature up, so most places actually felt too warm to him. The nippy night air probably felt good.

"Did the person who bought the book ever show up?" she asked the side of his face.

He kept his gaze out over the city. "No. Not that we ever saw. If they were there, they stayed inconspicuous. They didn't come out accusing the gallery owners of losing valuable property. There will probably be all kinds of insurance arguments after this, though."

"Weird the owner never made an appearance. You'd think after going to all the trouble of buying the book out from under the king, then taunting the king by inviting him to the gallery showing, that whoever is responsible for this would want to be present to see the king's face."

"I'd have assumed so. Maybe they thought it was safer to taunt him at a distance."

She snorted. "That shows a great deal of intelligence, if true."

He smiled softly, briefly, but he still didn't look at her.

She let the silence stretch, but only for a few moments.

"I haven't been avoiding you because I didn't want to spend time with you," she said, speaking as softly as his smile had been. Even with the echo of noise from traffic below and the wind whistling past, she knew he'd hear her. "But your father... The king..."

"He's complicated things because he keeps asking you to work for him."

"He has. For exactly that reason."

"I'll tell him to stop." He finally faced her.

The determined expression that hardened his jaw and set his mouth in an uncompromising line made her stomach dance. In a good way. Like freefalling off the side of a building, those moments before the harness caught and slowed her descent. Everything inside her tumbled around, chaotic and messy. A bubble of excitement and fear mixing together in her gut.

Breathless.

Sometimes Christopher looked at her like that and left her breathless.

"Will he listen?"

Christopher's jaw worked, like he was grinding his teeth. "I'll convince him. But..."

"But?"

"Are you certain? You've made a fair amount on these last couple of jobs for him. Do you really want to cut off that source of income?"

She raised her brows and for a moment wasn't sure what to say. Then she chuckled. Then she laughed. "I don't need his jobs. I'm perfectly capable of finding my own jobs. And I don't need the money. Anymore."

"There's a story in that anymore."

"There is." But not one she was going to talk about yet.

When she didn't elaborate, he nodded. "Still. He could be a very…useful benefactor."

"I don't need a benefactor. In fact, I'd rather stay off the king's radar all together. Breaking into his hoard was one of the stupider things I've done in my life. Before that, he didn't even know who I was." And that had been better. In a lot of ways, that had been better.

"If you hadn't, we wouldn't have met."

Which was the one thing she would have regretted. "It's not you that's the problem," she said instead because she was afraid of the implications of admitting she would have regretted not meeting him. "But you is… complicated."

"*We*," he emphasized, "don't have to be. *We* can just…"

"Just?"

He held her gaze and she couldn't have looked away if the building fell out from under them. Knowing that, even if it did, Christopher would catch her. How was she supposed to resist that?

"We can just go see a movie," he said after a moment. "Like we'd planned." His half frustrated, half hopeful shrug made her stomach flutter.

Well. And wasn't she used to taking chances? Didn't she *like* the thrill of not knowing for sure what could happen?

Usually, she didn't take that thrill-seeking, adventure-chasing attitude into personal relationships. But she also didn't allow many personal relationships that went past a superficial level. And she had a feeling, with Christopher, things were heading—maybe already well past— somewhere beyond superficial.

"Bit late for a movie," she said. It was after three in the morning.

A slow smile brought his mouth to life and that was impossible to resist, too. "Do you trust me?"

She almost gave the glib response. The one that should have been true. Instead, she gave him the real truth. "I do."

She didn't trust anyone. But she trusted Christopher. At least a little. She trusted him to catch her if she fell. And for her, that was a lot of trust.

He straightened away from her and snapped his wings out, the shift happening so fast it was if his wings had already been there and he'd just opened them. She was still learning about dragon shifters—had been doing covert research ever since meeting him—and she knew that not every dragon could do that. Not all of them could even shift partially so they had wings on a human body. A little less than half of them were capable of it. And even fewer of those could do the shift fast.

His wings stretched out behind him, glorious and huge, the thin purple membrane between the thick, hollow bones not quite see-through, but delicate enough she could see a series of veins, yet thick enough to tackle long distance flight without issue. The dusting of purple and yellow scales that crossed his chest and shoulders spread with his wings, almost like a cloak covering him.

Like this, it was impossible to pretend he was anything but what he was. And she liked that about him. She didn't have to pretend to be anyone else with him either.

"If you're up for it," he said, "I have a surprise."

She raised her brows. "I like surprises."

Without warning him, she jumped up into his arms. He caught her easily, as if he'd been expecting her, one of his arms secure under her knees, his other around her back. She liked this about him, too.

"Where to?" she asked.

"Short flight."

He dipped, then launched himself upward, the suddenness and stomach-dropping thrill of it making her chuckle. She tightened her arms around his neck. But not because she worried he'd drop her.

They banked out over the city, Christopher keeping lower than usual, flying in a slow tilt between the skyscrapers, moving along the street-carved canyons. They reached a building that rose several stories higher than its neighbors but was far from the tallest building in the neighborhood. From here, she could see out to the Hudson, and beyond that, New Jersey spread out in a series of low lights outlining the landscape.

Christopher could probably see the individual houses that made up all those lights. What would it be like to have that kind of vision?

As they lost altitude, she finally glanced down. A huge, flat patio beneath them stretched away from the top story of the building. The roof was a series of water tanks and some decorative stonework and wrought iron designed to hide those water tanks. The patio was a long, wide stretch of white stone circled by a red brick retaining wall that had actual gargoyles stationed at intervals along it. Plants spilled out of giant terracotta pots and long, narrow planters lining the base of the retaining walls.

As Christopher gently touched down, she saw the giant white screen stretched over the redbrick wall that led into the building. And in front of that, two huge and cushiony recliner seats pushed closed together, covered with thick blankets, and bracketed by small, marble and wrought iron tables already topped with popcorn. A thick pole behind the chairs had what looked like a projector fixed to the top. And beneath the tables, red coolers with white lids. The kind people used to take cold drinks to the beach.

She glanced up at him. She was still in his arms, and not in a hurry to get down, so she didn't loosen her hold on his neck yet.

"Where are we?"

"My home."

She raised her brows. "The one with the hoard?"

"No," he said with a deadpan. "Do not try to break into my hoard."

She laughed. "Aw, so I don't get a tour?"

For reasons that both delighted and confused her, an adorable blush crept across his strong cheekbones.

"You really need to learn more about dragon shifters," he said, his voice gruff.

"I'm trying." She narrowed her eyes. "What have I missed?"

"When a dragon shows someone their hoard voluntarily…? It means something. Most dragons only do that with their mate. Their long term partner."

She rolled her lips into her mouth and stared out wide-eyed at his patio so she wouldn't have to look him in the face. "Didn't realize that."

"I understand."

"Wasn't implying…"

"You don't need to panic about that now."

Panic? Yeah, that's what this was. Some panic creeping in.

But she was still in his arms, and this was his home, and she didn't want to panic now. She wanted to focus on this moment and not worry about what it meant or what might happen in the future.

Which meant a change of topic. "Is that a movie screen?" She nodded to the white rectangle sheet stretched over the redbrick wall.

"It is."

"Is it always there?"

"It is not."

"Set up for us?"

"I was hopeful."

She grinned. Her panic dying away, replaced by a race of tingles throughout her body. "You were confident."

"Hopeful," he said, a little twinkle in his blue eyes. The awkwardness of moments before gone.

"What's showing?"

"Old school rom-com. No heist movies."

She smiled softly. She'd told him no crime movies the last time he'd asked her to a movie—a date she'd proceeded to avoid because things felt…complicated.

This still felt complicated. It felt like things could get out of her control fast. She might like thrills, but she also liked control. She was used to controlling her life, used to answering to no one. With Christopher that was going to be a problem. And not just because his father liked to control everyone around him.

But for tonight, she wanted to forget that complication, too.

"I love a good rom-com. But it better be a real one. Not one that pretends to be a romance and then one of the romantic leads dies at that end."

He looked at her in genuine horror. "On what planet would something like that be called a rom-com? Where is the com in any of that? Or the rom?"

"You'd be surprised."

"No. Not in this house. Rom-com here means romance and comedy. Not…whatever else that is you just described."

She chuckled. "Okay, then. Old school rom-com with popcorn and… What's in the coolers?"

"Soda, water, and champaign. Wasn't sure what you'd prefer after a night's work."

Oh.

Yeah, this was definitely going to be complicated. That melty feeling in her chest didn't bode well. And yet, as her gaze dropped to his mouth, she decided this was the kind of thrilling fear she could definitely learn to live with. So long as she didn't think too hard about what was happening.

Still carrying her, he strode across the patio to the chairs. When he finally loosened his hold on her legs so she could slide back down to her feet, she went reluctantly, and didn't let go of her hold around his neck. This meant he had to lean over when she was on her feet. And this meant their mouths were remarkably close.

He wrapped his arms around her lower back,

tugging her closer, lifting her this time up onto her toes so they were pressed together.

That started a whole lot of tingles in her stomach and lower, and did nothing to fix the breathless problem. Not that she minded.

"Anyone else here?" she asked, her voice breathy and quiet. "Staff? Roommate?"

"No roommates. No staff."

"Now or ever?"

"Ever. Prefer my privacy."

She did, too. "So no one will interrupt. The movie."

His gaze moved over her face, down to her lips. "No one will interrupt. The movie."

"Good plan."

"Glad you approve."

"Should we…start the movie?"

He nodded. "In just one minute."

His mouth angled over hers, settling gently at first, a testing touch that gave her room to move, room to decide how much of a kiss this was.

She wasn't sure she made the decision consciously, or rather, this seemed like a decision she'd already made. Weeks ago. Right after they'd met. She tightened her hold on his neck, pressed harder into him, and let the kiss get serious, deep. Exploring what he offered of himself and returning a little of herself. His lips were soft, his hold on her hard. He tasted like the wine from the gallery reception and a flavor like heat that she couldn't quite describe.

One of his big hands crept along her spine and then cradled the back of her head, holding her close. Having his big body wrapped around her, feeling that heat and a strange combination of fear and security, sent a rush of warmth through her. Without his wings and scales, he felt like an ordinary man under her sensitive fingertips, his skin smooth, his chest hair soft. She traced a line along his shoulders, where the scales appeared when he had the wings. Studying the difference in texture. The similarity in heat.

His hand on her head remained a gentle cradle but the one on her lower back tightened, clenched at her shirt, and she found herself pressing even tighter against him. Wanting…more.

Dangerous. This whole thing was very very dangerous.

There were feelings here. And not just the physical, lusty, wouldn't-mind-getting-his-pants-off feelings. Emotional, personal feelings. The sort of feelings that made him blush and her get awkward just at the mention of mates. The sort of feelings that could be even more complicated than the situation they were already in.

And there was a part of her, a very serious part

of her, that was thrilled with that danger. With that possibility. With the rush of fear and adrenaline and terror.

She'd have to be careful of that part of her nature. Or she'd get in too deep too quick and get hurt. But…

But as he eased back, his breathing ragged, and set his forehead to hers, she closed her eyes and just absorbed the moment. Let his scent fill her. He had that faint smell of sugar cookies again. A yummy smell that made her hum.

Maybe this didn't have to end in heartache. Maybe this could be…something.

Or maybe she was a crazy adrenaline junky who was doomed to fall off a very high building attempting this.

Scarily, she felt absolutely positive, if she did fall, Christopher would catch her.

"So how do we start the movie?" she asked, letting humor and some of her lust into her voice to hide the deeper emotions.

His muscles loosened slowly, and his hold on her eased gradually, and after a moment, they both stepped back enough to allow some air to move between their bodies. She could still feel his heat, though, even when he wasn't pressed up against her.

"Remote," he said. He snatched a small, white,

rectangular remote she hadn't seen earlier off the table by one of the chairs and hit a button. The projector started, and the movie flickered to life on the screen.

She grinned and bounced into the recliner, shoved a handful of popcorn into her mouth as he sat. His smile was a little smug, but she could forgive him that.

"Do you always watch movies this way? I thought you said you went to matinees to avoid attention."

He pulled a can of soda from the red cooler under his table and cracked the top. "I do go to actual theaters sometimes. But I thought this would be better. After tonight's reception. And since it's three in the morning."

"Right. Good idea." She pulled up one of the thick blankets, getting cozy in her seat as the cold evening air brushed her cheeks. "This is better."

Privacy, a fun movie, popcorn and sodas. A little of the champaign as the sun rose.

And the company of someone she wanted to spend more time with. A lot more time.

Even if it meant tumbling off the top of that very tall building.

THANK YOU

Thank you for reading THE POISONS BOOK JOB! I hope you're enjoying the continuing tales of Myra and Christopher. I see this series as a little like a TV show, in episodes and seasons, and that aspect of it has been really fun for me as a writer. I hope readers are enjoying it too! Also, as might be obvious at this point, I've been heavily influenced by the TV show *Leverage*. So I suppose it makes sense that I'm viewing the series as episodes in Myra and Christopher's lives.

And things are getting very interesting.

The farther I get into the series, the more I see the framework of threads laid down for future stories, as well. So expect some things that feel like they end to crop back up again. As for Myra and Christopher's romance, yes, it's pretty slow burn. I like a good slow burn, though, and this one has been fun. Gets even funner (read in Elle Wood's voice), too. As the person who gets to see where all this is going, I feel like it's worth the wait.

For those looking to get the new stories as soon as they're available, from this book forward, at least through 2024, the novellas will be available at KatSimonsBooks before they release widely. So if you're the impatient type, be sure to pick the books up there.

If you prefer just getting emailed a reminder about the releases, or anything else to do with my books, please consider signing up for my monthly newsletter. All new subscribers get two free stories as well, one in my Cary Redmond urban fantasy series, and one in my Tiger Shifter paranormal romance series. There are also occasional excerpts, cover reveals, coupons to the store, and more.

You can also check out my website or store for updated news on releases, follow my author page at BookBub or your favorite vendor, or find me on Instagram and occasionally on Facebook.

Thanks again for reading!

~Kat

Don't miss the next story in
the Dragon Thief series!

THE VAULT JOB

Keep reading for an excerpt!

The Vault Job

Excerpt

ONE

Myra contemplated all the mistakes that had led her to this moment, staring down the barrel of a gun held by a very angry wizard inside a sealed steel vault. Everything that had led her here. Not every*thing*. Every*one*. One someone. One mistake.

One big, huge, fucking mistake.

A mistake she'd have to deal with later because now she had to prevent a panicking wizard from shooting her. Which was going to be complicated by the fact that they were both sealed inside this vault, and at any moment, they'd be discovered by shapeshifters. Who would be equally as upset to find Myra and the wizard inside the vault as Myra and the wizard were to *be* in the vault. And since those shifters had a problem with the wizard, and the wizard had a gun —currently pointed at Myra—none of this was good.

She didn't even have a convenient roof to leap off of to save herself. So irritating.

"You did this," the wizard hissed. "You did this on purpose."

"Get sealed inside a vault? You think I arranged *this*? To what end?" She wanted to search the area around the door, see if there was anything she could tweak to get the door opened again. But she couldn't move because gun in her face and angry wizard trapped with her.

"So they'd catch me. This was all a ruse. You're working with the shifters, aren't you?"

Not the ones he was referring to, but that was a technicality that could get her shot. "No. I am not working with these shifters." Absolutely true fact. "I would very much like to not get caught inside this vault by them. Or anyone for that matter. But I can't figure a way out of this while you're pointing a gun at my face."

"How can you get us out? We are *locked inside an impenetrable vault*."

"Yes. I am aware. But impenetrable is… Maybe not the right word here. Let's just call impenetrable a suggestion." At least to her. She had managed to break into some of the most impenetrable places in the city and its surroundings. That's what she did.

Also one of the things that had led to this mess. She'd never regretted that bet to break into the dragon king's hoard more than she did in this moment.

"What does that mean?" the wizard snapped. "A suggestion? No one can get out. We're trapped. If they find us, we're dead. If they don't find us, we'll suffocate. We're dead, one way or the other. If I shoot you, I can blame you. Someone might hear the sound and come get me out. And at the very least, I'll have more oxygen while I hope someone gets me out."

"But you'll be stuck in a tight space with a dead body. Not fun. Trust me. And anyway, if you shoot me, you have no hope of getting out of here without getting caught. I'm good at getting out without getting caught."

"You're caught now. I'd say you suck at it."

"*I'm* not the one who tripped the backup alarm that sealed the door shut." Though, she should have been watching this asshole closer to make sure he didn't trip that alarm.

She still wasn't entirely sure what had happened, how it had happened. She'd had her back to him for all of forty seconds. Next thing she knew they were both staring at the vault door as it slammed shut. And honestly, she'd had no idea a door that big and thick could swing shut that fast. It had taken a hefty heave to get it open once she'd unlocked it. Taken her and the wizard to move the huge round door to one side.

The instant the wizard—his name was Glen. A wizard named Glen. Instead of Astrid or Angelino or something. That felt strange to her—the instant Glen had triggered the backup sensors, Myra had taken one step toward the door, thinking she had time to keep it from sealing. Or at the very least, slip out before the three foot thick ode to engineering closed. She'd have been able to get it to open again from the outside. Maybe a little trickier. It was designed to seal in thieves until the authorities arrived. But she could do it. Wouldn't have been the first time either.

But then the door swung shut too fast for her to get out. So fast, if she'd tried, she'd have been flattened. Squashed dead between the door and the steel frame. Not an end she was excited about.

She didn't particularly want to be shot either.

"Listen," she said with as much patience as she could muster. "I need to examine the door. I might be able to tweak something. But I can't even attempt that while you're pointing a gun at me. So we need a little truce." She shrugged.

"Think of it this way. You can always shoot me later."

That thought obviously mollified him because, though he narrowed his already narrow dark eyes at her, he did lower the gun. Without the gun raised, Glen was a much less intimidating man. Wizards could be that way. Almost innocuous. Very ordinary and human looking. You couldn't just look at someone and assume they were a wizard—wizard was a gender-neutral term despite *some* people's insistence a wizard had to be a man. She'd met wizards who were women, who were nonbinary, who were transgendered, who were gender fluid. Gender had nothing to do with wizard magic. The term wizard applied to the *type* of magic someone wielded.

For example, she would never be referred to as a wizard because she didn't wield wizard magic. She had a different kind of magic. The kind that made breaking-and-entering a very successful career choice.

Glen, on the other hand, had a pretty decent amount of specifically wizard magic inside that wiry body. But it wasn't obvious.

He was taller than her, which wasn't hard, but not a giant. He was razor thin, even a little emaciated in his face, with sharp cheekbones and a narrow nose on which perched small, round, purely decorative glasses. In the right circumstances, he could have graced catwalks because he had that sort of haunted, interesting quality to his face. Not handsome. His eyes were too close together and his jaw too pronounced for handsome. But interesting enough she could see some designers wanting to drape him in their clothing.

He'd tied his long blond hair back into a low tail. And he'd dressed in black trousers and turtleneck for their heist, which was both a bit clichéd but also practical. She was wearing all black, too.

Not that the dark colors were going to save them inside a vault lit up so brightly she'd had to blink a few times when walking through the door.

While the interior of the vault was shockingly scentless, so without scent as to be noticeable even to her when she'd stepped inside, the stench of Glen's stress sweat was starting to permeate the air. That level of panic wasn't good for either of them. But at least he wasn't pointing a gun at her anymore.

"Don't try anything funny," he said, taking a step away from her. "I can shoot you before you can get the gun from me."

"I don't like guns anyway."

She really didn't. And never used them unless

absolutely necessary. In her line of work, it was almost never necessary. Guns were messy and made noise and drew attention. All the opposite of what she did or wanted to do when working.

Once she was sure Glen wasn't going to shoot her the moment she moved, she eased up to the vault door.

The interior of the vault wasn't huge. It was maybe eight by ten feet, lined with security deposit boxes, most of which were just filled with people's wills and family treasures—things like thumb drives with pictures and backup files. Very few would contain anything worth stealing for a thief and a wizard.

One of the boxes, however…

The reason the vault door was impenetrable was because all the family treasures and wills and miscellany belonged to shifters. This wasn't an ordinary security vault. It wasn't on the property of a bank, like human security deposit boxes.

This vault occupied space at the back of a law firms' offices in a mid-rise building in Midtown. A building that blended seamlessly with its neighbors, a couple of high and mid-rise, glass fronted buildings that held office space mostly. The building next to this one had offices on the lower levels and a hotel on the upper floors. Two different elevators. Not that she'd cased that building before.

Okay, she'd cased that building before. But that was just a coincidence. And had nothing to do with her current job. She'd cased a lot of the buildings in this city at one time or another. She was a busy thief.

The building with the law firm's offices was shorter than its neighbors by a few stories, but not enough to look awkward. The front was covered in dark brown, almost black glass, that reflected whatever sunlight got down the tunnel of the Midtown street. There was a coffee shop on the ground floor, and mostly lawyers and accountants in the upper floors, though one level was taken over by a budding new fashion designer's business.

She'd been tempted to sneak in there, just to see what the designer had for next season. Myra wasn't very into fashion for herself personally, but she liked the accessories that went with fashion and tended to keep up on the scene as a sort of side hobby, so she'd know what rich people were into at any given point.

The law firm with the vault was outwardly like any other firm in the building. Except that it was run by Shifters for Shifters—the non-dragon shifters. Dragon shifters had...other avenues of dealing with legal matters. But the average shifter in the city couldn't take advantage of dragon resources and had to do their own thing. The city tolerated shifters and wizards because they had little choice. Especially when the dragon king lived here. But that didn't mean they had to look out for the shifters.

This law firm, one Janu Peters and Schlotz, had an entire floor in the building to itself, and offered this vault for their clients' most prized possessions, because traditional banks could be bigoted toward shifters if they realized a shifter was a shifter. There were laws of course—that's why Janu Peters and Scholtz were in official business—but laws weren't always *helpful* in the ways one might think.

So she was currently trapped in a space full of things a shifter would love, inside a vault designed to withstand shifter strength—even dragon shifter strength—and to block most wizard magic. Wizards and shifters had a very mixed-bag sort of relationship. They either worked together well— with "well" being a subjective term because when they did work together that usually spelled disaster for other people—or they were enemies. There was very little in the way of neutral ground between them. Allies or enemies. No indifferent acquaintances. Ever.

In this case, she was dealing with a wizard whose relationship to shifters was…unknown. That made their position, trapped inside a shifter vault, particularly dicey.

She shouldn't have taken this job. She should have refused. She'd walked into the sort of job she *knew* better than to take.

But when the dragon king asks, it's so hard to say no.

Especially when you have a crush on, possible a budding relationship with, the dragon king's son.

Though, if Christopher knew where she was right now, and that she was here because of his father, he'd be so pissed.

She was pretty ticked off herself, to be honest. But that anger had to wait for later.

First, she had to find a way to crack open a vault from *inside*.

She'd never had to break out of a vault before. Usually, she was breaking into them.

Don't miss Myra and Christopher's
next exciting adventure.

THE VAULT JOB

Out now!

Join Kat's Newsletter

Stay Up-to-Date

On all Kat's News, Updates, and fun extras

New Subscriber Get Two Exclusive Stories Just for Signing up!

bit.ly/KatSimonsNewsletter

KATSIMONSBOOKS

Mystery

Urban Fantasy

Romance

And More!

KATSIMONSBOOKS.COM

The
CARY REDMOND
Series

GOT TROUBLE?

Don't Miss a Single Book in this
Action-Packed Romantic Urban Fantasy Series

Leopard Queens and Shifter Wars * The Trouble with Baby Gods and Vampires * The Trouble with Magic and Faery Curses * The Trouble with Wizards and Old Enemies * The Trouble with Death and Demon Gods

The Cary Redmond Series Box Set Books 1-3

Cary Redmond Short Stories

* When Cary Met Jaxer * When Cary Met Pickles * When Cary Met Marianne * When Cary Met Lucy * When Cary Met Angie * Cary and Deacon (Try to) Go on a Date * Date Night Take Two * Third Date's the Charm * Cary vs the Goblin King * Dinner with the Joneses * Cary and the Cursed Jack-O'-Lantern * Cary and the Demon Witch * Cary Goes to Hawaii * Cary Holidays * Cary and Dragons and Goblins * Cary's Galentine's Day * Cary at the Haunt and Howl * Cary's Leprechaun Troubles * Cary's Beltane Night Out *

When Cary Met the Good Guys (Collection 1)

Dates, Dinners, and Other Disasters (Collection 2)

Witches and Weavers and Ghosts, Oh Boy (Collection 3)

A Very Cary Holiday (Collection 4)

Romancing the Leopard: A Tiger Shifters-Cary Redmond Crossover Novel

Tiger Shifters Series

* Once Upon a Tiger * Along Came a Tiger * Here There Be Tigers * Her Tiger To Take * To Tempt a Tiger * Down Will Come Tiger * To Catch a Tiger * What a Tiger Wants * Taming Her Tiger

Tiger Shifters Series Vol 1 (Books 1 - 3)

Tiger Shifters Series Vol 2 (Books 4 - 6)

Seven Families Series

Wolf Family

Darkness in Stone

Redemption in Stone

Fated in Stone

Wolf in Stone: A Seven Families Box Set, Books 1-3

Demon Witch Series

Howling Dreadful

Moonlit Strange

Bone Lantern Witch

Spiderweb Witch

Storm Shadow Witch

Darkling Mist Witch

Joan of Kerry Series

Joan of Kerry: Joan and the Abhartach

Joan and the Leprechaun

Joan and the Kraken

Joan and the Selkie

Joan and the Goblins

Haunts and Howls Collections

Haunts and Howls and Guardian Spells

Haunts and Howls Where Demons Dwell

Haunts and Howls and Jesters Bells

*Tombstone Wizard * The Unshattered Sword *
Destiny Through the Cats Eyes * Going Out of
Business: Everything's for Sale * Anger Management *
Demonic Dates * Friday's Curious Shop * The Museum
of Small Art's Everyman * Burning Inside a Stone
Circle * Bored Questless * I Just Ate a Bug * Ting Ling
* Sophie Saves the World * Black Water Hawthorns
*To Dance in Fallow Fields at Midnight *

MORE BOOKS BY KAT SIMONS

Contemporary Romances

Designed for You

Poinsettias and Possibilities

Mystery and Thrillers

Ross and O'Neill Adventures

Galileo's Pendulum

Percy James Mysteries

Movies May Murder

Cookies Can't Crime

Diamonds Do Damage

Replicas Risk Ruin

Vacation Deadly: An Action Adventure Thriller
Collection

About the Author

Kat Simons earned her Ph.D. in animal behavior, working with animals as diverse as dolphins and deer. She brought her experience and knowledge of biology to her paranormal romance and urban fantasy fiction, where she delights in taking nature and turning it on its ear. She writes urban fantasy, contemporary fantasy, and paranormal romance in series which combine action adventure, the otherworldly, and a frequent dose of sexy romance.

The newest book in her bestselling romantic urban fantasy series about Protector Cary Redmond, The Trouble with Shifters and Fae Courts, sees a new direction for the intrepid Protector, her sexy leopard shifter mate, and the entire crew. Kat also launched a new novella length Paranormal Romance series that follows the adventures of a magical thief and the dragon shifter prince she just can't seem to shake—and really doesn't want to. The first season of the Dragon Thief series released throughout 2024.

Season Two begins in 2025 with The Crown of Kingship Job.

For something a little different, Kat also publishes fantasy, science fiction, and the occasional hockey romance under the name Isabo Kelly (https://www.isabokelly.com).

After traveling the world, living in places like Hawaii, Germany, and Ireland, Kat now lives in New York City with her family and a library's worth of books.

For more on Kat and her future books

Website: https://www.katsimons.com/
Newsletter: https://bit.ly/KatSimonsNewsletter

KatSimonsBooks

https://www.katsimonsbooks.com
https://www.TheCafeatKatSimonsBooks.com

Social Media

Facebook Page: https://www.facebook.com/
KatSimonsAuthor
BookBub: https://www.bookbub.com/authors/kat-
simons
Bluesky: https://bsky.app/profile/katsimons.bsky.
social
Instagram: https://www.instagram.com/isabokelly/
Threads: https://www.threads.net/@isabokelly